The Ocean
III

PALMETTO
PUBLISHING
Charleston, SC
www.PalmettoPublishing.com

Copyright © 2024 by Shelley Hibbard

All rights reserved

No portion of this book may be reproduced, stored in a retrieval system, or transmitted in any form by any means—electronic, mechanical, photocopy, recording, or other—except for brief quotations in printed reviews, without prior permission of the author.

Paperback ISBN: 979-8-8229-6037-4

The Ocean
III

Carry Me Through The Riptide

Shelley Hibbard

Chapter 1

Samantha sat watching another beautiful sunset. This was her favorite place to be. She loved waking up every morning to the beautiful view of the soft white sand, the gentle, soothing sounds of the ocean waves, and when the sun was setting, it was like it was kissing the ocean. She loved the sunsets, proving another beautiful day. She enjoyed going out and sitting in the sand every chance she could. She did her best thinking and planning from that perfect spot. She drifted from person to person. Her first thought always went to Jack. She had been in love with him for over thirty years now. It was as if they never had lost each other. Relocating to the beach had been a true miracle. To have found Jack again after all those years and that they still loved each other despite all the turmoil in her life recently. Oddly, after telling Jack that her oldest son was his, and then telling her son Nick that Jack, not her now ex-husband Victor, was really his father, Victor had entered their lives like a tidal wave. Victor had even held her and Jack captive at one point in her kitchen. Victor had accused Samantha of having something unbelievably valuable that had belonged to him. Thank goodness Kevin, Samantha's second son, had gotten there when he did to rescue them. Victor started taunting them all and then kidnapped Sabrina to try to get Sam to give him back an awfully expensive necklace. Victor's actions were very disturbing. She had learned that Victor had gotten caught up in a terrible insurance fraud. He faked his death in hopes to let the situation settle down before returning to his wife and family. Little did he know what he would be coming back to. Victor was not the loving husband and father she thought he was. The devil had gotten to him, and greed was hard to avoid for Victor. Jack had secrets too. She just learned he did not go to college on the football scholarship he had gotten in high school. He had gone into the military instead. She had never told Jack about their son because she did not want to ruin his opportunity to go to college on a full ride. Ironic, she chuckled to herself. Jack had promised to tell her about his military career soon. He had some of his retired military buddies help him to rescue Sabrina from the warehouse Victor had her held hostage in. She was so thankful for all their skills to bring her daughter home safely, but still, there were things she needed to know about his military life.

The sun was setting fast. The warmth on her face was fading. Her eyes were closed, and she was listening to the waves lightly crashing against the shoreline. It was New Year's Eve. It was going to be a magical evening. She was going to tell Jack that she was ready to marry him. She was going to finally tell him "Yes." Victor was in jail now. His trial would be coming up soon. But she was not afraid of him any longer. He was harmless now, wasn't he? She shivered at the thought. In the midst of her thoughts, Sabrina had yelled to her from the front porch of the beach house. Jack was just about done cooking dinner and asked her to help pick out the wine for the meal. As Samantha rose, smiling to herself, she knew exactly what wine she would pick for dinner. Her favorite,

Strawberry Sam. One that Jack had made and sold at his restaurant. It was light, sweet, refreshing and made her feel so warm, just like her loving family.

Chapter 2

Samantha took her glass of strawberry wine, raised it, and said, "I would like to make a toast." The lively conversations fell silent, and they all raised their glasses.

"Thank you to Jack for this delicious meal that you have slaved over all day. I must say, you are a better cook than me." Everyone chuckled and agreed.

"To my beautiful daughter, I am so thankful you are sitting here with us today, safe, and unharmed. To Freddie, thank you for helping Jack at the restaurant during the tragic events that occurred. It is heartwarming to have you join our family." Sam could not help but notice the look Sabrina and Freddie shared together. Just as she suspected, they were crushing on each other.

"And to my favorite youngest son and his fiancée Kali, I am so happy that you came home to share your engagement with us. We are all so excited for you and cannot wait for the wedding." Everyone started to sip their wine and Sam said, "Wait, I am not done yet." They all groaned and chuckled at her to hurry up.

"And lastly, I have some good news that I have been waiting to tell you all. We will be welcoming a new addition to our family," she paused, and said cheerfully, "in about seven months!" The room fell silent. Everyone stared at her, and Jack started choking. Sabrina was the first to speak. "Oh my god Mom, aren't you too old!"

"I am not too old, young lady," Sam laughed back at her. Sam looked over to Jack who was still coughing, and he looked pale. "Sweetie, can I get you some water?" she asked him.

Jack just shook his head.

Sam could not believe how quiet everyone was. Jack finally asked her, "Why couldn't you have told me privately?"

"Because Nick wanted me to tell you all when we were all together. With everything going on, it had slipped my mind. He wanted to be here, but they could not get the time off work, so he thought this would be a great idea."

Jack looked at her, puzzled. "Nick knew before I did?" he asked.

Samantha looked blankly at him and nodded her head.

"I can't believe I am going to be a sister at my age," Sabrina said.

"Wait, what! No, you will be an aunt, sweetie. You will be Aunt Sabrina," Sam giggled.

Jack practically yelled, "You aren't the one pregnant?!"

"Oh no, not me, silly. Nick and Sarah are expecting." Sam started laughing.

"Did you all think I was pregnant?" Sam said laughing with tears in her eyes.

She looked around the table, and everyone looked aghast. She suddenly burst into laughter. "I am so sorry you all thought I was the one pregnant. I was trying to tell it so you all would be surprised and excited for Nick and Sarah," she said.

"Well, I certainly was excited that the surprise was not you, but so happy for them." Jack grinned at her.

"Yes, that would be quite a surprise, huh? I am too old for that!" she exclaimed.

"I am glad it is not you too, Mom, which would just be weird. But I am so excited for Nick and Sarah. I am going to be an auntie," Sabrina said cheerfully.

"I agree, Sabrina. I think I would prefer to be an uncle rather than a brother," Kevin said. "Let's talk about something else, like the upcoming wedding," he said happily.

Everyone cheered at that and then all the talk was instantly switched to venue, colors, flowers, the *when?*, the *where?*

Jack was deep in thought as the conversation about Kevin and Kali's wedding engaged the group. He went back to that moment he found a positive pregnancy test in Sam's purse. He was frantically looking for Sam's phone and dumped her black hole of a purse on the floor and *surprise!*. He remembered breaking into a sweat in sheer panic. He thought of all the years he and his late wife Annie had tried to have a baby. All the treatments they went through with no positive results, ever. The thought that maybe Sam was pregnant had brought tears to his eyes at that moment. But with Sabrina's abduction, he could not give that even a second thought back then. He was overjoyed when he learned Nick was his son, not Victor's, but he did not raise him, either. He was not there throughout his life for ball games, helping with homework, talking to him about cars and girls. All the things dad and son do together. From the sound of it, he did not think Victor was around much for his children. Sam said he was a very consumed businessperson.

"Earth to Jack, hello Jack," Kevin said.

Jack looked at him and cleared his throat.

"Sorry about that. I was just daydreaming," he chuckled.

"No problem, Jack. We just wanted to let you know we have a theme for the wedding and a date and wanted to run that by you," Kevin said.

"Sure, what are your ideas?" Jack asked.

Kali excitedly answered they had picked the Saturday of Memorial Day weekend. The theme would be rustic chic. They were so thankful to Jack for letting them use his restaurant like he did for Nick and Sarah.

"It is your wedding day and you two can have whatever you wish, but what exactly is rustic chic?" Jack chuckled.

They chatted for hours about what it would take to achieve a rustic chic wedding at Jack's tiki bar and restaurant. They would turn his tiki bar into a country-barn area, with beautiful arrangements of sunflowers, and white sheer curtain panels to drape around the restaurant. He would work with the wedding planner to help with anything he could. Before they knew it, it was almost midnight. It was time to get the champagne and count down to the start of the New Year. They all gathered around the TV to watch the ball drop. They toasted the New Year and hugged each other good night. Sam and Jack stayed up to finish cleaning up.

"Enough, Jack, let's go outside and finish the champagne on the beach," Sam said as she grabbed his hand, and they took the bottle and glasses and ran to her favorite spot on the beach. They sat quietly for a while enjoying the crisp air, the twinkling stars, and the bright moon casting its glow on the water. Sam turned and looked up at Jack.

"It's so peaceful out here isn't it, Jack?"

He shook his head and pulled her closer.

"I have loved you for over thirty years. I cannot believe our paths crossed again and here we are together. I know we have a lot of catching up to do. We missed so many years together. There are secrets to share and stories to tell. But Jack, I want to take that journey with you, walk that path hand in hand with you until the day I die. I want to tell you, Jack, I am ready to say yes to you. I want to be your wife and live happily ever after with you," Sam said.

"Oh Samantha, I have waited so long to hear you say that to me. You just made me the happiest man alive! I know we have a few things to discuss but I promise you, I will always love you and be by your side, I will hold your hand forever and ever and promise to love you until the day I die. Thank you, my sweet, sweet Sam.," he said tearfully to her. He kissed her passionately, while the moonlight and the stars danced magically on the ocean.

Chapter 3

Samantha was sitting on the swing on the front porch. Her thoughts were as deep as the ocean. Reflecting on the night before, New Year's Eve, with everyone thinking that she was the one pregnant, she shook her head and giggled. As she sipped her coffee, she could hear Sabrina and Freddie inside, laughing over the pancakes that Sabrina was making. Freddie had come over first thing as he wanted to spend the morning with Sabrina before she headed back to school. The thought that Sabrina had to return to school brought tears to her eyes. She did not want her baby girl to leave yet. Because of her abduction, Sam wanted her nearby all the time. She needed to see her, hear her. Having her leave was going to be exceedingly difficult. Sam thought she had heard some hesitation in Sabrina's voice when she was talking to Freddie about having to go back. He was so thoughtful to offer to come over and help her pack her car up this morning. He too was probably having some issues himself, if she had to guess. Sam closed her eyes. The laughter from the kitchen, the quiet swoosh of the ocean, and the smell of the ocean filled her heart with warmth. She did not hear Jack walk onto the porch until he kissed her softly. She opened her eyes to see the most beautiful blue eyes staring at her. His handsome, strong face was looking deep into her eyes. Oh, how she loved this man.

"Good morning, handsome." She smiled up to him.

"Good morning my sweet lady." Jack said and kissed her again and then sat next to her and put his arms around her. She laid her head on his shoulder and smiled. This was so perfect, so right. She could not wait to have this every day for the rest of their lives.

Sabrina came out to the porch with Freddie. She handed Jack some coffee.

"Good morning, Jack." She beamed at him.

"Good morning, Boss," Freddie said.

"Good morning, love birds." Jack smiled back at them both.

Sabrina and Freddie just smiled at Jack. Everyone knew that they were crushing on each other, even Sabrina and Freddie.

"How is the packing going Sabria?" Jack asked her.

"Well, I am all packed, but not ready to go yet," she said sadly and looked over to Freddie. He was looking at her and holding her hand. He gave her a nod as if giving her permission. Sabrina looked at Jack and then to her mom. She took a deep breath.

"Mom, I have something I want to ask you. I have given a lot of thought. I am going to go back to school, but I want to transfer to someplace closer to home, here near the beach house. I want to be closer to you and to, well, everyone here." She smiled and looked over at Freddy.

Sam had tears in her eyes. She knew that Sabrina and Freddie had feelings for each other. There was nothing more that she wanted than her baby girl to be closer. But it had to be for herself, not for us, she thought. Sam got up and went over to Sabrina. She put her hands on her daughter's shoulders, looked her in the eyes, and asked, "Sabrina, sweetheart, I would love to have you closer, but you need to do this for you. Not for all of us. You have always wanted to be a pediatrician. Is that still your dream, your goal?"

Sabrina held her mother's gaze. She felt the love, she could see it in her mom's eyes. She smiled at her. She shook her head. "Sometimes your pathway may change, but the journey is still in reach. I still want to follow my dreams, but there is more I want to enjoy, more that I want to explore along the way. I do not want to disappoint you. I know how much you have wanted us all to do well. I just want to change my path a little bit. Will you be OK with that? OK for me to be closer to home, to be closer to you, be closer to what means most to me?" Sabrina smiled at her mom.

"Of course, Sabrina, all I want is for you to be happy. Never give up on your dreams. I know all too well; you should always follow your heart. It will never let you down."

Samantha and Sabrina hugged and cried. Sabrina then went over and embraced Jack.

"Well," she said wiping her tears. "I guess I should pack the car and up and head out. But I will be back soon, I am going to investigate schools closer to home."

Sabrina and Freddie went in to get her stuff. Sam sat next to Jack and put her head on his shoulder and sighed heavily.

"Well, that was something huh? But not totally unexpected," she chuckled. "I could tell they have feelings for each other. It is more than I thought."

Jack shook his head in agreement. "I could tell the way Freddie talked about Sabrina that he has real feelings for her. Are you OK with her coming home and looking for a different school? Premed is important."

"I am OK with it if she is happy and being true to herself. Let's go inside and grab more coffee while she gets her stuff together. It will probably be hours knowing all the stuff that girl brought home," Sam laughed.

Jack took her hand, gave her a squeeze, and led them into the house as Sabrina was laughing at something Freddie was telling her.

Chapter 4

It had only been a few days since Sabrina had gone back to school, but to Sam, it seemed like forever. Sabrina calls her daily with all her enthusiastic stories. She is looking extensively into other schools and cannot wait to get home. Samantha is patiently waiting for that day. She always wanted her children to be strong and independent, but after Victor had her kidnapped, she is constantly worrying about Sabrina. *Victor is in jail and no harm can come to her now*, Samantha says softly to herself. Samantha keeps busy baking and putting coffee on. Jack will be coming over shortly before he opens his bar. He thought it would be good to talk about some of the things that came about during Sabrina's abduction. She is curious about Jack's military career. All those years she thought he was in college on his football scholarship. The only reason she never told him about Nick was that she never wanted him to feel like he had to give that up, only to find out he gave it up on his own. She was deep in thought when Jack knocked and came in carrying some pink roses.

"Good morning, my sweet lady." He said as he pulled her close and kissed her passionately.

"Beautiful flowers for my beautiful lady," he beamed.

"Thank you, handsome man. You spoil me too much. But I just love them and you. Let me grab a vase. Help yourself to coffee."

Jack got his coffee and grabbed a blueberry muffin and waited for her at the table. She returned with the roses and put them on the table, gave him another kiss and grabbed her coffee and sat next to him.

They sat quietly for what seemed like forever. Jack finally cleared his throat, shifted in his chair, and said he would begin his story.

"I was so excited to get that full football scholarship. It was all I had dreamed of in high school. My parents were so proud of me," he said, staring down into his coffee mug. "But once I started it, it was not what I thought. I was not that person anymore. I really did not like the attention it brought to me. The hype of being a quarterback is just that, I felt like I was a robot, always being told what to do. Who to hang out with, what parties to attend and what cheerleader to date. I never felt like myself. I was not living my dream. I was living everyone else's dream. One afternoon, I just decided I was done. I was quitting. I never thought of myself as a quitter, but I could not stand the person I had become. I walked off that campus with my head held high. I got in my car, threw in my duffel bag, and drove. I felt so free. I wanted meaning in my life. I wanted to make a difference. I ended up at the local recruiting office. I felt so excited about it. I wanted to make a difference and joining the military felt exactly right for me. When I told my parents what I had done, I thought they were going to disown me. My dad was furious. You know, "my son," the famous quarterback on a full ride story. And what would his buddies at work think? And my mom, well she broke down crying hysterically. How could I do that? I could die. It's not for me. I am a football player, not made for the military, etcetera, etcetera."

Jack took a long breath and looked over at Sam. She reached out and held his hand, nodded her head to hear the rest of his emotional journey.

"I left three days later, off to boot camp. It was tough and grueling, but I was in decent shape from my football regiment, and I pulled through. I pushed myself. It was so gratifying. I went into the Special Forces and found my true self there. I loved the work and the adrenaline rush and that is where I met David, Wintt, and Scott. We were an unstoppable, dynamic team. We went through hell and back together and that is how I knew they would help us find Sabrina. We will always be a team, brothers until the very end."

Jack smiled. His memories truly made him happy and complete. He had truly found his calling in life.

Samantha squeezed his hand. He looked over at her. She had tears in her eyes. She got up and went to hug him. He held her tight. They said nothing for the longest time. No words needed here. Embracing said it all. She pulled away and looked up at him.

I have never been prouder and more honored to have you in my life now that I know about your true sacrifice and service to our country, especially knowing that you chose it over a football scholarship. I am so happy you followed your heart, lived your best life, and became the best person you could be. I just love and adore you, Jack." She kissed him softly.

"Thank you, Sam. That means a lot. I can't help but wonder what would have happened. If you had tried to contact me about Nick, I was probably overseas and I still wouldn't have been there for you. I have so many what-ifs with that situation," he said.

"I know what you are saying. Given all this latest information about your life, there are a lot of new what-ifs. But you know, Jack, we could what-if this forever? I am terribly sorry that I never told you about Nick. Something I will always regret. But looking back at your military career and the difference you made and continue to make as the amazing man that you became, I do not want you to ever regret or feel bad for that, OK?' she said softly.

"I only regret that I could not be the father I have always wanted to be. I could have had that maybe, just maybe," he said.

"Let's try to focus on the future and all the memories we will now make with all the kids, not to mention the grandbabies, too. I love you, Jack, and can't wait for our life together. Hopefully no more past skeletons will pop out of the closet now," Sam giggled. "Let's go for a walk along the beach. We can clear our heads with the fresh air."

Jack grabbed her hand and a bottle of wine, and they went out the door, down to the beach.

Chapter 5

Samantha loved walking the beachline down to Jack's restaurant. She was deep in thought. Kevin had called her, and they were talking about the wedding. Kali was so excited about the decorating plans. Her dream of rustic chic, or chic rustic, whatever that was, was coming together. Jack had reassured them his beach restaurant tiki bar would be transformed with lanterns, white sheer panels, all the flowers she wanted and lots of hanging lights. He would work with their wedding planner to achieve the perfect venue. However, he could not help the sand that occasionally blew in from the beach. Sam was excited to be helping at the restaurant today. Freddie had asked for a few days off, so she was going to help. Jack would have to run the bar; she was not a bartender by any means. She could not help but wonder if Freddie was going to visit Sabrina. Jack said Freddie has never taken any time off before. She was looking forward to working side by side with Jack. He genuinely enjoyed his customers, and she loved watching him mingle with them. It was the slow season now, so hopefully it would not be too busy of a day for her, Jack had told her. Because it would be mostly the locals there, he knew pretty much what they all ate and drank, so he would just stick to a menu with a few of the favorites. Her heart began to beat faster when the restaurant came into view. She picked up her pace. She could not wait to see Jack this morning. She loved seeing his handsome self. His blue eyes and great smile drew her in every time, he always melted her heart. She entered through the beach entrance and there he was behind the bar taking inventory. He looked up and gave her the biggest smile and walked over to her.

"Good morning, my beautiful, sweet Samantha." He leaned down to kiss her. He drew her into him and held her close. It was the best place to be, she thought to herself. The smell of his cologne was intoxicating. His embrace felt so good, so right.

"Good morning to you, my sweet, sweet man. How is everything going here without Freddie this morning?" she asked, looking up to him.

"It's better now that you are here." He beamed at her. "I am so excited to have you here with me today, the customers are so great, and I cannot wait for them to get to know you and you to know them. We are one big happy family here. Now let me run you through everything starting with greeting people to seating them to taking orders. We have two cooks today and one server that should work out simply fine because you, my sweet lady, are going to be perfect for this job. Everyone is going to just love you and you will be at ease," he said happily.

"Well, I think I will do OK, Jack," she chuckled. "I was a waitress when I was younger. I ran my household, raised three kids practically on my own. I think I got this." She grinned at him.

"I have no doubt," he said as he kissed her, took her hand, and led her into the kitchen to meet the staff.

Samantha felt like she was floating on air. She loved chatting with the customers, they were all so much fun like Jack had said. It really did feel like family here. It did not feel at all like she was working, she just seated people, took their orders, laughed and chatted the day away. Before she knew it, the place was thinning out. She looked at her watch and could not believe it was late afternoon. She had kept eyes on Jack all afternoon. He certainly was in his element here. People just loved him. How could they not? She giggled to herself. Jack came up behind her and put his arms around her.

"Hey, beautiful lady, would you like to take a break and have a bite to eat? I have a table ready for us," he whispered to her.

"Oh, that would be fantastic. I am starving." She grinned up at him.

Jack took her to a table in the back. The server, Brad, came right over with a bottle of wine.

"Thanks, Brad," he said. "Let Jon know he can cook us something now."

Brad gave a nod and off to the kitchen he went to help the chef.

"Well," he said to her. "How are you doing?"

"I am just loving it here. Your customers are awesome! I feel like I have been here years, not one day," she said laughing.

"I knew you would love it here and they would love you, too. You are a perfect fit here," he said.

"Thanks, Jack, for giving me the opportunity. I have not been in contact with this many people since my high school job of waitressing. It feels good, very gratifying," she said brightly.

"I am glad you feel that way. Let me ask you Sam, how would you feel about helping here two to three days a week? It would give you something to do now that Sabrina is back at school. It would give you a sense of accomplishment for yourself and we would be able to spend more time together," he said, raising his eyebrows to her.

The chef, Jon, came out at that moment and brought them each a steaming bowl of clam chowder. Samantha was so surprised by Jack's offer to work there; she could barely thank Jon for the soup as she just stared at Jack. She had so much love for him, she honestly thought she might explode with the excitement of working with him there.

"Sam, your silence is killing me over here," he chuckled.

"I am sorry, Jack. I was just so surprised and thinking about it. I am just so excited and happy and yes, yes, yes, I would love to work here. It feels so right, but only if I am not taking away a position from anyone else?" she asked.

"So here is what I have been thinking. I would like to slow down a little bit. I want to spend more time with you. I am going to ask Freddie to take over more of the management roles and fill in as bartender only as needed. If he is good with that, the rest of the staff is fine with the way it is. Brad helps Jon and the other chef out perfectly when they need him. They all work together like a well-oiled machine. They could run this place without me," he chuckled.

"You wouldn't be replacing anyone, just adding to the aviance, giving it the perfect touch," he said lovingly.

"Jack, I am so excited. I would just love it, thank you, my handsome man."

They enjoyed their meal together and finished the bottle of Strawberry Sam wine while excitedly talking about her working there. Before they knew it, the guys were saying good night and was Jack going to lock up the restaurant. Samantha looked around. All the customers were gone now. The restaurant was all clean and ready for tomorrow already.

"When, and how did that happen?" she laughed.

"See, I told you, they really don't need me. Only to give them a paycheck," he laughed. He took her hand. "Want to spend the night in the loft with me?" he asked her.

"I would love to, Jack. Thank you for the most wonderful day," she said, taking his hand and following him up the stairs to his private quarters.

Chapter 6

Samantha and Jack were walking hand in hand to the beach house. Jack did not need to be at the restaurant for a few hours yet, so he took the opportunity to walk Sam back to her house. They were deep in conversation about her working at the restaurant. As they were nearing the beach house, Sam noticed Freddie's truck in the small driveway. Hooked to the truck was a small U-Haul trailer. Sam gasped. She stopped and took in the sight. Sabrina and Freddie were trying to maneuver Sabrina's dresser through the front door. They both were laughing so hard they could not carry it. Sam looked up at Jack with tears in her eyes.

"My baby girl is home," she said.

Jack squeezed her hand.

"I think they could use some help," he chuckled.

When Sabrina saw her mom and Jack, she set her part of the dresser down and ran to her mom.

"I am home, I am home for good," Sabrina squealed.

"Oh sweetie, I am so excited to have you home, I missed you, what a delightful surprise this is. I had no idea what Freddie was doing on his day off. So did you find another school?" she asked, hugging her daughter.

"Yes, I did. I wanted to surprise you by coming home and saying that I transferred to another college. It was hard to keep the secret. Freddie was worried about taking the day off from work, he said he has never missed a day," she giggled.

"It was hard to keep the secret from Jack. I do not take time off, so when I asked for it, Jack looked worried, but could not tell him why. So now you know, boss." Freddie smiled at Jack.

"I admit, I was worried, but figured if you needed to tell me anything, you would. But this is a great surprise, Freddie. It will be nice having Sabrina home. I know Sam is beyond grateful for you bringing her home." Jack walked over and hugged Freddie.

"Thanks, Jack, that means a lot," Freddie said.

Sam went over to Freddie, hugged him too and said, "Thank you for packing up her stuff—Lord knows she has a lot, hence the U-Haul behind your truck—and for bringing her home. I feel so relieved that she is closer to me. After her abduction, I worry about her more than ever," Sam said.

"Well, let's get this stuff inside," Sabrina said. I will have a lot of unpacking to do. Mom, is it ok if I also use the other extra room?" Sabrina asked batting her eyes to her mom.

"You can use it, Sabrina, as long as it all fits in there," Sam chuckled. The four of them spent the next hour unloading the truck and U-Haul. Jack needed to get back to the restaurant, since the lunch crowd would be there soon.

"Hey, I need to get to the restaurant Sam." He said.

"Jack, I can drive us back if you want. I can leave the U-Haul here and the girls can finish unloading it," Freddie said.

"Well, if you want to stay and help Sabrina, I could have Sam go back with me for the afternoon. You can come down when everything is settled here? What do you say, Sam, are you up for another day at the restaurant?" Jack asked.

Freddie and Sam looked at each other and both nodded their heads in agreement.

"Sounds great to me." Sam beamed.

"Sounds good to me, but only if you are OK with it, Sam? I know you covered for me yesterday and would not want to overwhelm you with helping cover me?" Freddie asked.

"Freddie, I don't mind at all. I really enjoyed myself yesterday. The day just flew by," Sam said.

"Tell you what," Jack said, "why don't you and Sabrina come down to the restaurant and join us for dinner? We can catch up on things then.

"Perfect, we should be done by then," Sabrina said enthusiastically.

"I doubt it, but we will be there anyway." Freddie smiled at Sabrina.

Sabrina just laughed and ran to the U-Haul to grab more boxes.

"Good luck with her, Freddie," Sam giggled.

"Let me go change real quick, Jack, and I will be ready in a few minutes," Sam said.

Sam changed quickly. Sabrina came in and hugged her mom so tight.

"I am so happy to be home, Mom. I hope you are not mad that I did not tell you at first?" Sabrina asked Sam.

"Don't be silly, Sabrina. I am over the moon that you are home. I love surprises. I am so grateful to Freddie for helping you get back home. If you need a little more space to house all that crap you brought home," Sam chuckled," you can use the shed, and the small sitting room off the back of the house. I don't really use that room because I love the ocean view off the front of the house. I haven't been in that room in months."

"OK thanks, Mom. Oh, and by the way, why are you changing your clothes?"

"Never mind you," Sam said, brushing her daughter away.

"Love you, Mom," Sabrina giggled, and ran out to continue moving her stuff. Her mom was right, she had a lot of crap, she laughed to herself.

Chapter 7

The day flew by again for Sam. She loved greeting people. She enjoyed the lively conversations she had. There were some people she wanted to sit down at their table, grab a glass of wine and laugh and talk away the afternoon with. But she remembered she had other tables to attend to. She was genuinely enjoying this job.

Jack was watching Sam from behind the bar. She was laughing with a couple that were regulars there. He loved her laugh, her face said it all, she looked so happy. She honestly enjoyed what she was doing, and making the regulars feel really at home with her warm, beautiful personality. Sam was walking over with another order for Jack.

"Hey, handsome. Can you fix me a gin and tonic and a glass of Chardonnay please?" Sam said, grinning at him.

"Anything for you, lovely lady. Looks like you are having fun with the patrons, huh?" Jack chuckled.

"Oh, yes. They are all just super people. I have fallen for Mr. Smithfield. He ordered the chowder again today with bourbon on the rocks. I am thinking this is his usual?" she asked Jack.

"Bingo, you got it. You are picking up on their habits on day two. Very impressive, my lovely waitress. Here are your cocktails, now get back to work and stop flirting with the staff." He winked at her.

Sam put the drinks on her tray and sashayed her hips as she delivered them, leaving Jack shaking his head and laughing.

The crowd was thinning out a little bit. Sam realized the rush was over, she looked, and it was three thirty already. She saw Jack at the bar, went over and sat on a bar stool.

"Phew," she spoke. There were a lot of people here today. Most of them were locals, right?" She beamed at him.

"Yes, they were. But you knew that because I saw you talking to every one of them." He smiled at her.

"Well, I wouldn't want to be rude now, would I?" She winked at him.

"Of course, we would not want that. We need those patrons; we love those patrons." He smiled. "So, I was thinking once Sabrina and Freddie get here, we can tell them about our plan to have you work here a few days a week and Freddie do more of the management end for me. Are you good with that, Sam?" he asked her.

"Absolutely. I am so excited about working here. And of course, spending more time with you, my love," Sam said lovingly.

"Well, I am glad to see where your priorities are, love. But seriously, I thought it would work out perfectly," he spoke.

"I agree. You know, there was another idea I wanted to run past you, Jack. I was thinking about our living conditions. I was thinking of asking you if you wanted to move into the beach house. But now that Sabrina just moved back home, I am rethinking the living arrangements."

"Oh Sam, I have thought of that idea every day. I hate being apart from you, that is why I thought having you work here a few days a week would help fill that void in my heart," he said, taking her hand.

Jack heard someone clear his throat. He turned and saw Mr. and Mrs. Smithfield standing there smiling at them, holding out their check.

"Oh, sorry about that, Charlie," Jack said. "Let me take that and get you some change."

"No, no. The change goes to our lovely new waitress here. She is just a sweet, beautiful young lady. We enjoy talking with her and hopefully we will see some more of you young lady." Mr. Smithfield smiled, took Sam's hand, and kissed it.

"Oh Charlie, stop flirting with her. She won't serve you anymore if you embarrass her," Mrs. Smithfield said, whacking his arm.

"Thank you for the compliment. I enjoyed talking with you two and look forward to bringing you soup again tomorrow." She smiled at the adoring couple.

"Oh, that is wonderful dear. We look forward to tomorrow then. Good day," Mrs. Smithfield said, as she took her husband's arm and shuffled to the door.

"They are the cutest couple, Jack. How old are they? Does he still drive?" Sam asked him.

Jack laughed. "God, no, he does not drive anymore. They are in their late eighties. They have a taxi bring them and pick them up every time. It is usually Tony. Sometimes he waits for them, sometimes he comes in grabs some lunch too. Especially in the cooler months. He is a pretty nice guy. Almost like a son to them," Jack said.

"Oh, that is so endearing. They are the cutest couple. I hope that you and I will have that in our later years too," she spoke.

"Oh, I don't think Tony will drive us all over, honey," Jack said laughingly. "But I do believe our love will last forever and ever. Do you want a glass of wine, Sam? I have your favorite right here," he said, pouring her a glass of Strawberry Sam.

"I would love a glass. Thank you, Jack," she said.

"Sit and relax for a minute. I have a few things to do in the kitchen. Come get me if you need me, OK Sam?" he said.

"You got it, boss." She smiled with a hand salute.

Sam sat there enjoying her wine. A few more patrons came up with their checks, had cash for her and told her to keep the change. She thanked them all and told them how she loved chatting with them and could not wait to see them again soon.

She heard Sabrina and Freddie come in. Sabrina's laughter gave them away. She turned to see them hand in hand. They truly looked like they were in love.

"Hey, mom, drinking on the job I see," Sabrina laughed at her.

"I never get to drink on the job," Freddie said shaking his head at her.

"I will go check things out in the kitchen. That is probably where Jack is, right?" he asked Sam.

"Yes, he is back there, he left me in charge out here." Sam grinned at Freddie holding up her wine glass.

Freddie laughed all the way to the kitchen.

"Mom, what are you doing?" Sabrina laughed at her.

"Just taking my break. Jack poured me some wine. I love it here, Sabrina. The people are just so fun to meet and chat with." Sam told her all about her day and how sweet Mr. and Mrs. Smithfield were.

"I am so glad you are having fun, Mom. I am happy you are going out and meeting people. I think this is a great fit for you. Not to mention you can spend more time with Jack." She smiled at her mom.

Jack and Freddie came out of the kitchen.

"You ladies ready for dinner?" Jack asked. "Let's grab some drinks and head to a table. Brad and Jon are plating up our dinners now."

"So, while we are waiting for our food," Jack began, "there was something we wanted to run by you two."

Freddie looked at Sabrina and they both shook their heads.

"Sam has really been doing a fantastic job here at the restaurant. She is so good with the patrons, and they seem to love her a lot. So, I have asked her to work here three to four days a week. She would greet and seat everyone and take orders. Freddie, you could still run the bar, but I would help you out a little bit more because I would like you to take over some of the management responsibilities. That way, Sam and I can spend more time together. Does that sound good to you, Freddie? Would you be up for learning more about the management part?" Jack asked him.

"Wow Jack, that sounds really awesome. Are you sure you want me though?" Freddie chuckled.

Jack laughed and said, "I think you run this place better than me now anyway."

"It would be my pleasure and honor to help you out more with the restaurant. Thanks so much, Jack." Freddie stood up and hugged Jack.

"Food's ready," Jon said as he and Brad brought out steaming plates of roast beef, and mashed potatoes, with all the fixings.

"Oh, this looks delicious. Thank you," Sam said to them both.

Jack brought over a bottle of wine and the four of them enjoyed a wonderful evening talking about the restaurant and Sabrina relocating to a closer college that was just the next town over. Sam was so excited to hear she was going to be so close to the beach house. The start of the new year was going perfectly. Sabrina had relocated and continued her education. Kevin and Kali were getting married, and Nick and Sarah were going to have a baby. This was going to be a fantastic year. Nothing could break their happily ever after she thought to herself. Everything was perfect. She smiled as she looked around and joined in the laughter.

Chapter 8

The next few weeks flew by quickly. Sabrina settled in at the new college and was busy with that. She spent her spare time with Freddie. Samantha was enjoying working at the restaurant. She would work at least four days a week. She enjoyed it so much. She also loved being around Jack more. They were finding a comfortable routine. Freddie was a natural with the management responsibilities Jack had given him. Jack enjoyed tending bar more now, and absolutely loved laughing at the stories people had for him as he poured their favorite cocktails. Valentine's Day was fast approaching. Jack was busy with Freddie organizing drinks and food specials. The theme of love and romance filled the air. Sam was excited to help with the decorating. Jack asked her if she wanted work that day as it would be busy, and she would be an immense help. She jumped at the chance. Being around Jack would be the greatest feeling but also to be surrounded by people celebrating love would be enchanting. Sam was assembling the menus when she heard someone come into the restaurant. They weren't due to open for another hour yet. Sam was surprised to see Jack's lawyer, Bob, walking in. The look on his face told her something was not right.

"Hey, Sam, how are you?" he asked her.

"Good to see you, Bob. Well, I am not sure it is good to see you. The look on your face tells me this is something other than a social call. Never good to see one's lawyer just show up," Sam said nervously.

He nodded at her. "Jack around?" he asked briskly.

"Yes, he is in the back with Freddie. I will get him for you," she said quickly.

"I need to speak to you both privately," he spoke.

Sam nodded and ran to the back. She busted through the door. It startled Jack and Freddie.

"Sam, what the heck, you scared the crap out of us. What has gotten you so anxious?" Jacked asked, going over to her, and putting his hand on her shoulder.

She took a deep breath. "Bob is here and wants to see the both of us privately. I can tell by the look on his face, something is wrong, very wrong, Jack."

"Oh, did he say what he wanted Sam?" he asked.

"No, but like I said, his face looks tense, there is something wrong, Jack."

"OK, let's go see what he has to say, Sam. Be back, Freddie." Jacked put his hand on Samantha's back and guided her into the dining room where he saw Bob pacing the floor.

"Hey, Bob, what's going on?" Jack asked shaking his hand.

"I have been OK, Jack. But today, today, not so good. Can we go somewhere we can talk privately, please?"

"Sure, let's go to the back of the restaurant. We don't open for another hour. Do you want anything to drink, Bob?" Jack asked his friend, who was pale as a ghost now.

"No, I am fine, thanks, Jack."

They walked to the back and sat at a table in the corner. Bob started taking out a stack of papers. He sat down and just looked at the files in front of him.

"Bob, please tell us what the hell is going on. You are making me anxious here," Jack said, shifting uncomfortably in his chair.

"There is no easy way to tell you, so, I will begin at the very beginning. Just hear me out and then we can go over everything with details. "

Jack looked at Sam; he took her hand. Whatever Bob had to say, he could tell it was not going to be good.

Bob sat upright and took a deep breath and began the story he wished he did not have to tell. This was going to crush them both, and he hated this for his dear friends.

"About two weeks ago, there was a small fire at the prison where Victor was housed. It was deliberately set. It was in the activity room. I know what you are thinking, how come it was not on the news? They were keeping it secret because of the ongoing investigation. There were five men who lost their lives in the fire." He stopped there and looked over at Jack and Sam. He could see the panicked look on their faces, and tears starting to run down Sam's face. He hated himself for having to go any further.

"Yes, as I was saying," he cleared his throat to continue the horrific story. "Five men perished in the fire. They had to use dental records to verify the men. Sadly, Victor was one of the men in the activity room then. But…" he did not get to continue because Sam began to weep. Jack got up and pulled her into his arms and held her tightly. Bob gave them time to process this news.

"Jack and Sam, I have more I need to add to this," Bob said softly.

"Isn't that enough for now, Bob? This is just shocking news, and I am not sure how much more Sam can hear right now?" Jack asked painfully.

"No, please sit down, Jack. There is something more I need to share."

Jack and Sam sat down. Sam's body was quivering uncontrollably and she wasn't sure how much she could hear at this point. "The medical examiner has double-checked the following information, but the body believed to have been Victor's did not come back with that identity match. His name was Vincent, same last name as Victor's," Bob said as kindly as he could.

"I don't understand this," Sam cried. "Victor isn't Victor, but someone named Vincent is Victor?"

"I know this is very confusing and frustrating, I took the liberty of hiring a private investigator before I came to you with this crushing news. The prison is also conducting their own investigation and the DA's office is all over this as well."

Sam just cried and cried. Jack did not know what to say. He was just as stunned and completely in shock too. He got up and told them he would be right back. He told Freddie to put up the closed sign and grabbed the bottle of bourbon and three glasses and returned to the table. Jack poured them all a drink. He shot his down first. Bob appreciated the calming from the bourbon burn.

"Do you two have any questions for me?" Bob asked them both. They sat and looked bewildered at him. "I will leave you to process this, and I will be in touch with you as soon as I have any updates from the private investigator and the prison officials themselves. I only ask that you only tell those closest to you who need to know, for now. I am so sorry I had to deliver this kind of disturbing news to you, Sam. I will let myself out," Bob said, shook Jack's hand, and headed for the door.

Freddie stood listening at the kitchen door; he could not believe what he was hearing. His knees were shaking, and his heart was beating so fast and loud he was sure Jack could hear it in the dining room. Samantha and her family had been through so much grief and aggravation with Victor; how could they get through this ordeal and what would they have to actually go through if this man was not really Victor? Freddie's mind went to Sabrina. Poor thing, he thought. This is going to send her into orbit. He grabbed his phone and texted her to come to the restaurant. He told her to use the beach entrance. Being that he had already put up the closed sign, Sabrina would panic as soon as she saw that coming in. He wanted to spare her as long as he could.

Freddie rushed over to the table as soon as Bob left.

"Hey, Jack, and Sam. I am so sorry about what Bob just told you about that fire in the prison. I was listening at the door. I knew it was going to be unwelcome news, and I could not help myself. I had to eavesdrop," Freddie said sadly.

Sam took Freddie's hand. "This is just so unbelievable. I feel numb, and my mind is whirling with so many thoughts, what-ifs and so many questions. You have no need to apologize for eavesdropping. Freddie, you are like family and that means a lot that you were concerned enough to want to listen. I need to call Sabrina. She needs to hear this bizarre story about Victor or whoever the hell this man is, oh God, this is insane." Sam said holding her head.

"I took the liberty of texting Sabrina for you, Sam. I did not mention anything to her. She is on her way now. I told her to use the back entrance. I locked the front door and put up the closed sign," Freddie mentioned.

"Thank you, Freddie. You are so thoughtful," Sam said, hugging him.

"I let the cooks go but I will find a little something for you guys to eat, you are going to need some nourishment." Freddie said, turning to go to the kitchen.

"Freddie," Jack called to him.

"Yeah, boss."

"Thank you." Jack smiled at him.

"Come back to the table when Sabrina gets here, that way we can all be together as we relive this nightmare when we tell her," Sam said to Freddie as he disappeared into the kitchen.

Chapter 9

Sabrina was walking with a slight skip down to the restaurant. She was taking the beach down. She loved this as much as her mother did. She loved the peaceful feeling. She always felt so free, not a care in the world. Nothing can bother me here, she thought. She was so happy she moved here to be closer to her mom, and who was she kidding, Freddie as well. She could feel her face flush thinking about Freddie. He made her laugh, he listened to her, and just made her feel warm and happy all the time. I may be falling in love, she giggled to herself. She picked up the pace. She was excited to see Freddie this afternoon. She was surprised by his text message to come earlier than planned. She was only working on some research for her paper anyway. She enjoyed the break from it. She loved it, but sometimes it was overwhelming. She would be happy to be a physician, maybe she could be content being a PA, who knows she thought. Just roll with it, she told herself. She had nothing but time on her side to help her make her decision. And just like that, she could see the restaurant. The tiki bar would soon be open for delicious drinks. She was excited to sign up for the beach volleyball tournaments Jack had there. Now that she was living at the beach house, she could be around more to have some fun. Sabrina looked past the tiki bar up to the restaurant. She could see her mom and Jack in the window looking at her. She smiled and waved to them. She was so excited they were waiting for her; she ran the rest of the way to the back door where Jack was waiting for her.

Samantha held her daughter tight. She did not want to let her go. She did not want to have to tell her this bizarre story about her dad. She did not want to tell her daughter; she did not want to crush her heart again over Victor.

"Hi, Mom," Sabrina sang joyfully. "I am so glad to see you and Jack. Freddie texted me to come over, we planned to get together later but," Sabrina suddenly stopped talking and looked deep into her mother's eyes. Just then, Freddie came out of the kitchen, walking so calmly, like slow motion. Where was the bright smile that he always had for her? She jerked her head to Jack. He looked concerned. Sabrina felt the blood drain to her toes. Something was wrong, very wrong. She shivered and looked back to her mom. Sabrina could tell she had been crying. Oh god, what has happed now she said to herself.

"Let's all sit down," Jack said softly.

Freddie went over, gave Sabrina a quick hug, and held out her chair for her. She nodded and tried to smile back, but felt so anxious, she was frozen.

"I can tell by all your faces that something is very wrong. Please do not sugarcoat it, tell me the truth. I know you probably think I have been through so much recently with Victor kidnapping me, holding you and Jack hostage in your kitchen, and then trying to kill you both, but I am stronger now, Mom, please tell me what it is," Sabrina said with tears in her eyes.

"I know you are stronger, sweetheart. I just hate to tell you the terrible news, it breaks my heart knowing that it is going to break your heart," Sam said, taking Sabrina's hand. She took a deep breath and began.

"Jack's lawyer, Bob, stopped in with this very bizarre story. He explained that there was a fire in the prison that housed Victor. Five men perished in that fire."

"No! No!" Sabrina began to cry.

Freddie held her tight. "Hang on Sabrina, there is more you need to hear, honey," he whispered to her.

Sabrina wiped her eyes, took a deep breath, and nodded as her mother continued.

"Bob said they had to use dental records to identify the men. The problem they ran into is the body they thought was Victor's, had dental records that belonged to a man named Vincent, with the same last name as Victor's. There isn't more at this time because it is an active investigation and the prison, and the DA wants this on the down-low until they can figure out the bizarre situation. Bob has hired a private investigator to investigate this for us," Sam said taking a much-needed deep breath.

Sabrina sat there, frozen it time. She was confused with her feelings for Victor as it was. He was her dad, but he had done some terrible things to her and her family. Should she be crying, or should she be celebrating? She could not feel any particular emotion, she sat frozen in time. She looked at Freddie, at Jack, and then over to her mom. They were all giving her time to process this, and waiting for her reaction, her questions. She was stunned and did not know what she should say.

"Sabrina, honey, it is OK. I know this is hard for you, but please say something. Please tell me at least what you are thinking," Sam said softly to her daughter.

"Mom, I do not know what to say. I don't know if I want to cry or what. I hated Victor, my dad, for all the evil he had done to us all recently. But if that man was not really my dad, then I should not feel that way. I actually hated a man that I didn't even know."

"I don't know where Victor is, honey, or anything about this man named Vincent. I don't know if this story is real. It is just such a crazy story. We must wait until we hear back from the PI Bob hired," Sam said, trying to convince herself as much as her daughter that everything would be OK, and they should just go on like nothing ever happened. Yeah, like that was even going to work, she thought.

"You OK Sabrina?" Freddie asked her.

"I have so many mixed feelings. Would it be OK, Mom, if I walk the beach with Freddie while I absorb all this and can figure out how I really feel?"

"Of course, Sabrina, that sounds like a good idea, I may end up doing the same thing with Jack shortly." Sam stood and gave her daughter and then Freddie hugs.

Jack came around and pulled Sam into his chest, holding her tight. He could feel her taking a deep breath and relaxing some. She stayed in his arms for what seemed like forever. She felt mentally and physically exhausted. She wanted to walk on the beach, but she didn't think she had it in her. So, they stayed in that night, trying not to let this get the best of them.

Chapter 10

The next seventy-two hours where the longest Sam had ever lived through. She tried to keep busy at the restaurant. Sabrina had classes but she was zombielike in everything she did. Sam had to relive the ordeal two more times as she called Nick and Kevin to tell them what she knew. They both were deeply concerned for her and Sabrina's safety. With Victor's whereabouts unknown they shared their concern for their safety. Samantha didn't say it, but she had those exact feelings.

Valentine's Day was in two days. Sam didn't feel the love in the air like she used to. They all were going through the motions preparing for Valentine's Day, a special, special evening at the restaurant. Sabrina said she was going to come and help too. Sam was glad to hear she would not be alone. Sam was busy putting together the special menus for Valentine's Day dinner when Freddie came up to her. He stood there for a few minutes saying nothing but looking like he needed to talk.

"You want to sit, Freddie?"

He nodded and sat next to her. "Thank you, Sam. I hope you don't mind, but I asked Jack to come in here and join us?" he said nervously.

"Of course I don't mind, Freddie." She smiled at him, just as Jack came in, hugged Sam, and sat next to her.

Patting Freddie on the back he said, "What's up, young lad?"

He looked squarely at Sam, drew a much-needed breath of encouragement, and said nervously, "As you know, Sabrina and I have been spending a lot of time together, and if you did not notice," he smiled meekly, "she is a very special part of my life now. She makes me laugh, she makes me smile, she makes me so happy. I knew right away I would marry her. You are probably thinking we haven't known each other that long, but I know that I love her. I would like your blessing as I want to propose to her on Valentine's Day. I know with everything going on it may not seem like the right time, but I have been planning to ask her to marry me on Valentine's Day, I think she would find it very special." He smiled at them both.

Samantha could feel the tears rolling down her cheeks. She knew that they had a connection. Freddie was an amazing young man. But he was right, they really hadn't known each other that long. But did that really matter? She and Jack knew right away that they were in love and sadly they didn't follow their hearts. She wanted better for her daughter.

"Sam, honey, are you in there?" Jack said, touching her arm.

She smiled and said "Yes, yes, I am. I was just thinking about our young love many, many years ago." She turned to Freddie. "Freddie you are right, you haven't known each other very long but I can see the love you have for Sabrina every time you look at her. I can tell she loves you too. I was remembering how I fell in love with Jack in just a short time. Neither one of us acted on those feelings. I want you and Sabrina to have your happily ever after. You have my blessing, son." She stood to hug him.

"Thank you, Sam. I promise I will always love your daughter. She means the world to me," he said hugging her back.

Freddie went back to work feeling on top of the world. He was so excited and couldn't wait to propose to Sabrina on Valentine's Day. Keeping this a secret from her was hard. He caught himself many times wanting to just ask her, but he really wanted to give her the perfect place and to have her mom and Jack there, that would make it even more special. She was his everything and he couldn't wait to give her everything that he could.

"I am so happy for Freddie," Jack said to Sam as they were going over the menu for Valentine's Day. "He is such a good person. He works hard, he is polite to everyone, and he is on a good path in life. Marrying your daughter is the icing on his cake Speaking of marriage, we need to start thinking of our own wedding. Have you given any thoughts on when you would like to get married, my sweet, sweet Sam?" Jack asked her lovingly.

"I think about it every day, Jack. Just when I think about talking to you about planning our wedding, something gets in my way. This ordeal with Victor has most of my attention. The other half of me now wants to focus on Sabrina. She will be over the moon happy when Freddie proposes to her. Then there is Nick and Sarah's baby coming, and Kevin and Kali's wedding. I don't know when to squeeze us in," Sam said laughing.

"Yes, you are right Sam, there is so much going on. I shouldn't have even asked. I just love you so much and I cannot wait to marry you and spend the rest of our lives growing old together."

"Thanks for understanding, Jack. Let's table it for now but I promise you we will be married soon."

"That is good enough for me, Sam, I know deep in my heart we will get married. I promise to wait for you as long as it takes. Let's get through Sabrina's engagement and this mess with Victor. I wonder where Freddie and Sabrina will get married?" he said grinning ear to ear.

"I can only think of one perfect place Jack." She smiled and hugged him closely.

"That would make me so happy," he said, closing his eyes and holding her tight. He never wanted to let her go.

Chapter 11

Sam woke to songbird-like singing. She could hear Sabrina getting ready down the hall. She was always so happy. She could only imagine how ecstatic she would be later today when Freddie proposed to her at the restaurant. Freddie had it all planned out. He wanted to propose before they opened. He said he would be too nervous waiting all day. Sabrina said she was already going to come down and help, so Freddie had asked her to come earlier so she could help decorate. Little did she know the decorating was already done. It would be so perfectly set for a wedding proposal. Sam went down the hallway toward the beautiful voice. She stood there for a moment taking in the sight of her beautiful daughter. She was so proud of the young lady she had become and so elated about her future. Sabrina was on a good path.

Sabrina turned and jumped. "Mom," she squealed, "you scared me," she said, grabbing her chest and laughing.

"Good morning, beautiful daughter," Sam said, hugging her.

"Good morning, beautiful Mama." She hugged her back.

"You haven't called me that in years, sweetie." Sam beamed.

"You will always be my mama, but I figured now that I am a college student, it's more grown-up like if I call you Mom or Sam," she said, giggling.

"Mom is fine, Sabrina dear. I am going to make coffee and some breakfast. What do you want this morning, Sabrina?"

"I think I will have some yogurt. Freddie said the menu is full of delicious meals and desserts, so I will save my calories for later, thanks, Mom."

"Anything for you, Daughter." Sam smiled at her and turned to go downstairs to the kitchen.

Just as she was making coffee there was a tap on the door. Sam went to find Jack standing at the front door peeking in the window by the door. She grinned at his sweet face trying to look through the windows. She opened the door to him and found him holding the most beautiful bouquet of pink roses.

"Jack, those are so beautiful! Come in here so I can hug and kiss you madly," she said, beaming.

"Happy Valentine's Day my sweet, sweet Samantha. I love you more today than yesterday and twice as much tomorrow. Please be my Valentine forever."

"Oh Jack, you are adorable. Of course I will be your forever Valentine. Thank you for the beautiful roses, they are exquisite. You spoil me," she said winking at him.

"I love to love you and spoil you, Sam," he said, hugging her and kissing her cheek. Her face was buried in the roses, or she would have kissed his sweet lips.

"I was just about to make some breakfast; can I make you anything, Jack?" she said, headed to the kitchen to find a vase for the roses.

"I will just have some coffee for now, thanks. I thought I would come over and spend some time with you this morning. We will be so busy later with the..." but before he could say *engagement*, Sam hushed him quickly.

"Sabrina is upstairs getting ready. She'll be down shortly; we can't spoil the surprise, Jack," Sam said quietly.

"I know, Sam. I was going to say restaurant and feeding all those lovebirds," he said, laughing.

She grinned and sat his coffee on the table for him. She sat and joined him.

"Thanks for coming this morning and bringing me flowers, Jack. I did not expect it at all," she said meekly.

"I know those are the best surprises when you don't know about them, Sam. Plus, it's cold and rainy. I figured you would want to walk the beach to the restaurant, but I don't want my Valentine to get all wet and melt away."

She swatted his arm. "Oh, you are so full of it this morning. I love it, don't stop," she giggled.

Sabrina came into the kitchen looking like a perfect Valentine. She had on a red sheath dress, red shoes, and purse. Her hair was smooth and shining from being straightened. Her makeup was simple with a touch of red lip gloss. Jack whistled at her. "Don't you look beautiful, Sabrina. Happy Valentine's Day, dear." He got up and hugged her.

"Thanks, Jack. Happy Valentine's Day to you too. Why are you here so early?" she asked, and she then noticed the beautiful pink roses.

"Oh, those are beautiful. Let me smell those." She lifted them off the counter and took a deep breath. "Oh, they smell heavenly," she sang out.

"Where are the vases, Sam? I will get one for you so you can put them in water already," Jack said.

"I think they are in that cupboard over the stove. I can't reach them, so please grab whatever you can find, Jack."

Jack went over to get the vase down; he opened the cupboard and there were about four of them in there. He took one that was a beautiful, heavy one.

"This one will do, don't you think?" he asked, turning toward Sam.

She looked at him and smiled. "Yes, that is beautiful. Actually, I don't remember that vase. Sabrina is that your vase?" Sam asked her.

"No, Mom, not mine. It's beautiful though. It looks very expensive."

As Jack was carrying the vase over to the table, there was a clanking noise that came from inside, like broken glass pieces hitting each other.

"Oh god I hope I didn't just break this!" Jack yelled.

"What was that, Jack? Sounds like there are glass pieces in there," Sam shrieked.

Jack looked inside. "Oh, it's like those glass stones people used to put in vases, I think," he said, shrugging his shoulders and handing the vase to Sam. She looked at it oddly. She shook it a little bit then tipped the vase to see the crystal-like stones in the bottom. It was difficult to make them out, so she reached in to pull some out. She retrieved a handful and pulled her hand out. She looked at Jack and then over to Sabrina and said "Oh my God, oh shit, oh noooo," she cried. She quickly sat down holding the vase and the crystals. Her hands started to tremble.

"Those are pretty crystal stones to use for vases," Jack said laughing.

"Jack, I don't really think those are what we thought they were," Sabrina said, shaking her head and rushing toward her mom. They sat there looking and staring for what seemed like hours.

Jack noticed Sam looking very pale all of a sudden, so he said, "I don't understand what is happening here. Can someone fill me in on this vague decorating item?"

Sam turned slowly, looked up at Jack and said quietly and breathlessly, "These are not the stones you use in flowerpots or vases, Jack.

Look at them," she said, as she pulled her hand up and displayed a very stunning expensive crystal necklace.

"Holy shit!" Jack screamed.

"I know, I know," Sam said.

"Mom, do you think this is what Victor was searching for, or whoever the heck that man is?"

Sam could only shake her head; this couldn't be real. They had searched this house looking for whatever it was that Victor had left behind that landed him in prison. But Victor wasn't that man in that fire, so who was portraying her ex-husband? Sam felt her world crashing in on her, she felt warm and cold at the same time, she felt nauseated. She looked up at Jack to try to say something, but no words formed, before she felt herself go limp.

Sam woke to Jack sitting next to her on the sofa holding her hand and a washcloth on her head.

"Oh dear, I've done it again haven't I?"

"Yes, Mom, you fainted again," Sabrina said as she held the washcloth on her head.

"You OK now, Sam?" Jack asked her.

"Yes, yes, I am fine. Just a little embarrassed. I seem to faint when I get a little bit uptight, don't I?"

"Luckily, I recognized your symptoms and caught you before you face-planted on the floor. Sabrina grabbed the vase and that exquisite necklace before they hit the floor too," Jack chuckled.

"Oh my god, did they break?"

"No, no we caught them, Mom. So, do you think that's what Victor, or should I say Vincent, was looking for? That is one beautiful necklace," Sabrina said wide-eyed.

"I have a very sick feeling, dear, that the necklace is the answer to that whole mess. Jack, who do we call and what do we do with it now?" Sam suddenly thought aloud.

"Well, it is Valentine's Day. It's going to be a very busy, wonderful day down at the restaurant. I say we bring the vase and necklace with us, and I will put them in the safe at the restaurant. They will be safe there until tomorrow when we can manage this situation. Would that be OK Sam? I don't want anything else to ruin this beautiful day."

She smiled at him in agreement. "This is going to be a beautiful day and we won't let Victor or whoever that impostor is, ruin our day."

"Good. Now go upstairs and finish getting ready. I will call Freddie to let him know why we are delayed and that we will be down there shortly, OK?" He winked at Sam.

"I will hurry, I promise. Sabrina come help me with my hair, OK, sweetie?"

"Absolutely Mama. Let's get you ready for Valentine's Day." She beamed at her mom.

Chapter 12

Freddie watched anxiously out the window for Jack's Jeep to come into view. He couldn't believe what Jack had told him about finding that necklace in the vase, and of all the days. They certainly didn't need to add any more drama on an already very confusing, stressful situation where Victor was concerned. Or whoever that guy was. He felt a little sad for Sabrina. She didn't know her dad when she was growing up. He was never home, she had told him. Then her father supposedly dies in an airplane crash. But suddenly reappears, kidnaps her, and tries to kill Sam and Jack over something he says he left behind, that Sam now has stolen from him. He lands in prison, dies in a fire, but now they have discovered it was not Victor's body according to the dental records. Sabrina really doesn't have a father. She has never had one and now who knows where her real dad even is. With their upcoming engagement there would be the thought of who would give her away at the wedding. He knew in his heart she probably would ask Jack, but he felt sad for her to have all this despair for a man she never knew. And there she was, his beautiful wife-to-be. Jack was helping her and Sam out with an umbrella over them both. Jack was a true gentleman, no doubt. He truly admired that man and hoped he would be just like him. He took a deep breath and headed over to the front door to let them in. The best day of his life was about to begin.

"Happy Valentine's Day, Freddie." Sabrina ran to him and, on her tippy toes, she kissed and hugged him tightly.

"Happy Valentine's Day, Sabrina. You look absolutely beautiful in red." He held her close. He loved the smell of her hair. Her perfume was a soft scent of vanilla, she smelled delicious. Freddie hugged Sam and shook Jack's hand.

"So, are we all ready for the special day?" Jack bellowed out to Freddie.

Freddie felt his face flush. The place looked so beautiful already.

"I thought I was coming down early to help decorate?" Sabrina asked Freddie.

"Well, that's true hon, I did do a lot while waiting for you, so why don't we go into the dining room and try one of the special drinks I have on the menu?"

He took her hand and led her into the dining room. It was decorated with roses; fairy lights adorned the walls. Candles and flowers were at each table. Red tablecloths were accompanied by white folded napkins. The lights were dimmed low. There was soft music in the background.

"Oh, wow, Freddie. This is so beautiful and romantic. The patrons are going to love it," she said, looking around and taking in the hard work he had put into every detail. She turned to him to inquire about the special drink he promised her. Freddie was on one knee. Flowers in hand.

"Sabrina, love, you have made me the happiest man on earth. I love spending every minute I can with you. You make me laugh. You make me smile; you give me so much love. I love it when we sing together even if we are off key. Whatever we do, it is so right, so perfect. I love you with all my heart and soul and I would be so honored if you would be my wife." He pulled the ring box from his pocket and opened it for her.

Sabrina was crying tears of joy; her hands were shaking. He was hoping this was the element of surprise and love and not one of sure panic and remorse.

"Yes, yes, yes! I will marry you, Freddie!" she squealed. "I have loved you since I first saw you. You make me happy every time I look at your adorable smile. I love our adventures and spending time with you, and I would love to spend the rest of my life having new adventures with you. I would be so honored to be your wife," she said so joyfully.

Freddie put the ring on her finger. He kissed her and held her tight. He felt the tears welling up in his eyes. He loved her so much. He was so happy and relieved she said yes.

Sabrina was so excited. She couldn't believe the surprise proposal. Freddie was her everything, he was her rock. She couldn't believe he wanted to marry her, and the ring was so beautiful. She needed to look at it again. She stared down at her newly blinged ring finger and cried more. It was an exquisite engagement ring.

Jack and Sam went to hug the happy couple. "Congratulations! We are so happy for you!" they both shouted. They were all hugging when Jon brought in the champagne and Brad had chocolate covered strawberries to celebrate the special occasion.

This was such a magical day. Sam and Sabrina greeted and seated the customers. They enjoyed the friendly conversations. Sabrina caught Freddie smiling and winking at her all day while he was busy with the cocktails behind the bar. The day had flown by with all the excitement. She couldn't believe how lucky she was. To think that her mom and Jack knew and helped kept the secret from her too. It took a lot of hard work and she appreciated everyone that helped. After the last of the customers left, Jack put up the closed sign on the door. Now, it was their time to enjoy the special day. He grabbed Sam's hand, nodded to Freddie. He dimmed the lights and grabbed a bottle of champagne. He took Sabrina's hand, and they all went to a table in the back corner. Jack had secretly been back there preparing their table while Sabrina and Sam were enjoying the customers.

"Oh, wow, Jack, this is so beautiful," Sam exclaimed, giving him a quick kiss.

The cooks brought out a family style dinner. Jack told all the staff to go home. They had a long productive day with delicious meals for everyone. Jack poured them all some champagne.

"I would like to make a toast to Sabrina and Freddie. Congratulations on your engagement. Love has brought you two together for a lifetime, one that will be full of joy, happiness, and love. Enjoy your new path together. Cheers." They all toasted each other. "And may I add, to my special Valentine, Sam, you are my sweet, sweet Sam. Thank you for being the beautiful person that you are. Cheers."

The evening was full of lively conversations talking about Sabrina and Freddie's plans for their upcoming wedding. Sabrina was talking a mile a minute about dresses, the when, the where, etcetera. They all laughed and enjoyed her bubbly enthusiasm. They talked about Kevin and Kali's upcoming wedding as well. Maybe they could have a surprise baby shower for Nick and Sarah then too. There were so many happy things coming up. Sam sat thinking of how blessed she was. But then the mess with Victor/Vincent creeped into her mind. She could feel the tears rolling down her cheeks. She didn't want these terrible thoughts in her head. This was a special day. She quickly wiped them away and took a deep breath.

"Mom, are you OK over there? You're crying," Sabrina said sadly.

"Oh, I am, I am just fine, sweetie. She just so happy, these are tears of happiness, that's what they are." She smiled at her daughter.

Jack took her hand. He knew what she was going through, and she was probably putting on her happy face for her daughter. He knew tomorrow would be another stressful day. He would have to call his lawyer about the necklace they found in the vase. That meant the FBI would be coming for a visit. He hated that they would have to go through all of this, but hopefully it would all be over soon so they could enjoy all the upcoming events.

Chapter 13

Samantha woke to her cell phone ringing. It was Jack and it was only eight o'clock in the morning. He was sorry to wake her but ironically his lawyer Bob had messaged him, and he had info for them from the PI on Victor's case and would be at the restaurant at nine o'clock. Jack told her he would send Freddie down shortly to get her and Sabrina and bring them to the restaurant. He mentioned they could tell Bob then about the necklace and the vase that they had found. He signed off with several hearts and "I love you. Stay strong."

Sam rolled her eyes and fell back onto her pillow. She knew this had to happen, but she was dreading it. She got up slowly and she replied to Jack. She walked down to Sabrina's room to wake her. She opened the door. Her sweet daughter looked so peaceful, and so happy. Her red dress she wore the night before hung over her chair, her shoes and purse on the floor. The red roses Freddie had given her smelled beautiful from her nightstand. And there was the beautiful velvet box that held the engagement ring that had brought all the love and excitement from the night before. The beautiful memory, she thought. She took a deep breath and sighed.

Sabrina rolled over. "Mom, why are you standing in the doorway staring at me like that?" She said half laughing. She sat up. "What's the matter, Mama?" she asked Sam.

"I was just reminiscing about last night. It was such a beautiful day, wasn't it?

"It was the best day ever. I can't believe I am engaged to the most amazing man," Sabrina squealed. "I am the luckiest girl in the world."

"You're the second luckiest girl, because I am the luckiest girl in the world," Sam giggled back at her. Sam sat at the edge of the bed. "But seriously, we need to get up and get ready quickly. Jack is sending Freddie down shortly to pick us up and take us to the restaurant. Jack got a message from his lawyer, Bob; he is going to meet us all at the restaurant at nine o'clock this morning. He has info for us from that PI that he had hired for us, so let's get up and get at it," Sam said standing up.

"Oh, this day is going to be shitty!" Sabrina wailed.

"Sabrina!" Sam called over her shoulder, shaking her head at her charismatic daughter's language.

"Well, Mom, it is true. I hate that we have this BS—there is that better?—to go through." She smiled at her mom.

"Yes, better. It is true, total BS, dear. Now get up and get going; your fiancé will be here soon."

"I love the thought of that, my fiancé. Woo-hoo, I am so lucky." She jumped up and down on her bed.

Sam laughed inside herself all the way back to her room. She loved her daughter's wit. Sometimes she was an adult and then in a blink of an eye, she was still that sweet, loving, alluring little princess.

Sam was in the kitchen when she heard a knock on the door. "Come in, Freddie," she yelled.

"Good morning, Sam," Freddie yelled out as he came in.

"Good morning, Freddie. No need to knock, that door is always open for you," Sam said as she hugged him good morning. "We're almost ready. You want coffee to go, Freddie?"

"I would love a cup, Sam. Black, please."

Sabrina came full throttle down the stairs and ran right into Freddie's open arms. It was so invigorating to see such young love, Sam thought.

"Good morning, fiancé," Sabrina giggled at Freddie. "I just love the sound of that."

"Good morning, my beautiful fiancée." Freddie grinned back at her." I love that too, Bri."

"Bri?" Sam questioned.

"Oh, that's my…" Sabrina started to say.

Sam cut her off and said "TMI. I do not really need to know, I guess," she laughed, walking away. "Grab your coffees and let's roll."

The restaurant was less than two miles, but it seemed like twenty miles to Sam. There were only three traffic lights and they hit them all in red, which dragged out the less-than-short ride. When they pulled in, she noticed Jack in the doorway, and he was letting Bob in. Oh boy, this was getting so real, she thought to herself. Her palms were sweating. Freddie opened her door for her to help her out and ran to help Sabrina out thereafter. He was such a thoughtful young man, Sam thought. Jack came to her and hugged her tightly. He knew she would be so nervous, he needed to give her strength.

"Good morning, love. Sorry I had to wake you this morning with such shitty news," Jack said.

Sam chuckled. "You sound just like Sabrina; she said the same thing. It's so true, but let's just get this over with. I am so curious with the info he has found out." Sam gave him her best smile.

They went into the restaurant and followed Jack to the back where Bob was getting folders out of his briefcase. It felt weird to Sam, to be at the exact table where they had celebrated her daughter's engagement less than fifteen hours ago. Sabrina is right, this is just shitty, she thought to herself. She smiled to herself, feeling a little bit better. Bob shook everyone's hands and asked them to be seated. Jack reached over and took Sam's hand and gave her a reassuring squeeze. Jack noticed Freddie had done the same with Sabrina.

"Good morning, everyone. So sorry to spring this on you so suddenly, but I figured that you were all anxious and hesitant at the same time in learning about this bizarre situation regarding Victor. So let me read the report that my PI sent to me.

"The report is a result of the investigation of the above-named Victor who allegedly died at the fire at the prison. Dental records were used to identify the men who perished in the fire. The medical examiner's report stated that the dental records used to identify Victor did not match. They matched that of Vincent with the same last name. So here is where the truth and lies are explained. Victor and Vincent were identical twins. Birth certificates are enclosed. Both boys went to boarding schools together. However, when Victor and Vincent's parents divorced when the boys were twelve, according to school records, Vincent was expelled due to unruly behavior. Vincent was enrolled in another boarding school, who accepted a very large contribution from their father. Vincent remained at that school until graduation at age seventeen, as Victor graduated from his school, same year." Bob paused and took a deep breath, looked at everyone, as they were wide-eyed and shocked, and continued on. "The report continues as such. I researched and have supporting documents for all the above and the following:

"Victor did perish in that plane crash several years ago. However, Vincent learned of his twin brother's death, and decided to take over his identity. Vincent had spent several years in and out of mental institutions under a false name. It appears he had a rough childhood and young adult years. Large donations were given to this institution until the death of their father. Vincent then left the institution. It is believed he used Victor's name and reputation to get by in life, lying and stealing as he went along. Fast forward, you encountered him most recently last fall when he came to see you looking for something of value that he had hidden in your possession because the walls were closing in on him." Bob stopped. Everyone was looking earnestly at him. Sam was white as a ghost. Sabrina looked shocked.

"Let me get some water." Jack jumped up to go retrieve it, but Jon was already bringing it out and Brad followed with bourbon and glasses. Jack couldn't be more grateful for the latter. Bob was the only one that took the water. They all quickly shot one back. Sam took a deep breath.

"Victor never mentioned having an identical twin brother. How could he not share that?" Sam questioned.

"There was a lot of jealousy on Vincent's part. The boys were constantly in competition with grades, sports, etcetera. One of the reasons Vincent was transferred. He always felt that Victor was better at sports, more intelligent and powerful. So, Victor probably didn't care to talk about him because to Victor he didn't exist. They had no contact with each other since they were separated at boarding school. Vincent never showed up for either of their parents' funerals," Bob said.

"So, are you saying that Vincent took over my dad's identity after the crash, and no one knew this?" Sabrina asked Bob.

"Yes, and he was able to stay under the radar. He moved to a small town out west. No one knew of Victor there."

"This is so bizarre, Bob. I can't believe he got away with using Victor's identity for so long without anyone noticing," Sam said, shaking her head.

"So, Bob, we have to tell you something that we just recently found out yesterday." Jack began the story of finding the vase with the necklace in it.

Bob quickly got out his phone, sent a text, and said the FBI would be there within the hour Yup, Jack figured that they would, but not this quickly. Bob asked if they could take a break as he needed to make several calls with this new development. They all were happy to take a break. They needed to get their strength back before the FBI got there and drilled them again about finding the necklace in the vase. Sam took a deep breath. Hopefully, this will all be done quickly, and they can all move on to happier times, she thought to herself.

Chapter 14

Sam sat on the beach watching the sunrise. This was her favorite place to be. She could always clear her mind and feel refreshed. The last two months had been a whirlwind. The prison had released the story of the fire and the men who had perished in it, which brought to light the story of Victor and his identical twin brother Vincent's story. That was a nightmare. So many old friends had reached out to her, she could not relive this bizarre story every time. Thankfully she didn't have to tell the story of how Vincent stole Victor's identity after his death, because of his childhood jealousy of Victor, the news took care of that for her. She was thankful to be living at the beach. She felt like she was hiding from the world right now. Sam could sense Jack walking her way, she could smell his cologne and hear his soft shuffle on the sand. She stood and embraced him and took in his strength. She loved being wrapped up in his loving arms.

"Good morning, my sweet Sam, what a greeting," he said, and kissed her.

"Good morning, my love, you are a wonderful way to start my day."

"So, on that subject, how would you feel about us living together? We should move in together, Sam, so we can have this every morning. We should also set our wedding date too." Jack grinned at her.

"I agree, Jack. Now that all this craziness has settled, we should focus on us. Whenever we try to set a date, something comes up. Let's go back to the beach house and set a date," Sam said enthusiastically. They entered the house and immediately heard Sabrina laughing. She was FaceTiming Freddie. She waved at them both and continued chatting with Freddie. Sam made some coffee and they sat together at the table.

"So, you think we should move in together, Jack?" Sam asked.

"I think it's long overdue, Sam," he laughed quietly.

"Well, your place over the restaurant isn't big enough. And I'm not sure here is the right place with Sabrina here and all."

"Do you know if Sabrina has mentioned when they want to get married?" he asked.

"No, all she said was soon."

"OK well here is what I was thinking, Sam, I know you love this beach house. I want to keep us here on the beach too."

"OK, that's a good start." She smiled at him.

"Did you know that Mr. and Mrs. Smithfield, the sweet couple from the restaurant, are selling their lovely beach home?"

"No, I hadn't heard that, tell me more, Jack," she said excitedly.

"So, it's a lovely remodeled, two-story house, it has five bedrooms, three bathrooms, and all the updated cabinets, appliances, etcetera."

"It sounds too big for us." Sam said.

" Well, it's big enough for our families and grandbabies to come visit us whenever they can." He beamed at her.

"Oh, Jack, that is perfect. When can we go look at it?"

"Well, I took the liberty of making an appointment for us this morning."

"Oh, Jack, you're amazing, this sounds so exciting, when?"

"About an hour. Let's finish our coffee, let me make us some pancakes and we will go. Sound good?"

"It's perfect, Jack. Thank you."

Sabrina came dancing in. She was definitely on cloud nine. She was glowing.

"Good morning, Parents," she sang. Jack and Sam quickly looked at each other and smiled.

"Good morning, Daughter," Jack quickly said.

"Good morning, Daughter," Sam said, smiling.

"What are you and Jack doing this evening?" she asked.

"Well, it is Monday, so the restaurant is closed today, so I guess that means we have no plans. You have any plans, Sam?" Jack asked.

"Nope, I have none. What are you thinking, Sabrina?"

"Freddie and I have been doing a lot of thinking about our wedding and maybe we can go over some of the plans with you two? He is coming over shortly. We are going to go through some of my bridal magazines, then we are going to make homemade pasta and sauce for dinner. Sound good?" she asked them excitedly.

"Sounds like an enjoyable day for you two. Dinner sounds delicious. But, Sabrina, I didn't know you could make homemade pasta and sauce," Sam teased her.

"Oh, I can't, you are right, Mom. But Freddie is an amazing cook. He said he learned a lot working at the restaurant with Jack. "

"Well, we would love to have dinner with you two. Sounds like a nice evening, Sabrina. Tell Freddie to stop at the restaurant and bring down some wine from the bar when he comes, OK?" Jack said.

"Great, I will let him know. So, what are you two doing today on your day off?" Sabrina asked.

"Funny you should ask, but we do have some exciting plans. We are actually going to look at a beach house that is for sale up by the restaurant. The Smithfield house for sale." Sam said.

"Oh, wow that's fantastic news. It's about time you two find your own home together. I hope it is everything you are hoping for," Sabrina said. "What will you do with this house?"

"I haven't given it a second thought. Jack just mentioned the house thing this morning, but we do want to get our own place if not now, very soon and we want to set a wedding date too."

"Oh, how exciting, Mom. Do you have a time frame yet?"

"No, but like you, very soon," Sam laughed at her daughter.

"Well, I will go call Freddie and tell him to grab some wine from the restaurant. You two have fun looking at the house. See you later." Sabrina hugged them both and danced her way out of the kitchen.

Sam giggled to herself. That girl was such a bright shining star. She was always so vibrant and happy.

As soon as Jack pulled up to the house, Sam fell in love with it automatically. It was a beautiful buttercream color with soft turquoise accents. They walked up the seashell sidewalk holding hands. Jack gave her hand a squeeze and she smiled at him as the Smithfield's opened the door to welcome them in. They had spent several hours with the dear, sweet, elderly couple, from the tour room by room to the back patio, complete with outside furniture and kitchen area. It was the view of the ocean that captured Sam's heart, as it always did; she knew this would be their forever home. One to welcome family and friends. She was beginning to think that life for her and Jack could finally exist.

Chapter 15

Sam and Jack walked into a delicious smelling house. Freddie and Sabrina were cooking together in the kitchen. Bridal magazines and a planner book were on the table. A bottle of wine was open. This was such a sweet sight, Sam thought. She loved seeing her daughter so happy; with all the craziness lately, she deserved to be happy.

"Hey, guys, it smells delicious in here," Jack said.

"Hey there. Thank you, we are having fun. Freddie taught me how to make the sauce—that went fine, but the pasta not so good," Sabrina laughed.

"You did good. It will get easier with more practice," Freddie said to her.

Sabrina rolled her eyes at him, "Yeah right," she laughed.

They all laughed at that.

"So how was the house, Mom?"

Jack poured them some wine and smiled at Sam. Sam held his hand, beamed at them, and said, "It was absolutely beautiful. It was everything we wanted and more. So, we put in an offer, and they accepted it," she squealed delightfully.

Sabrina immediately jumped up and down, the pasta spoon still in her hand. Sauce went flying. They all laughed so hard at her, Sam had tears in her eyes.

"What will you do with this house?" Freddie asked.

"Well, we don't know exactly what your plans are, but I was hoping that you and Sabrina would take it."

"Oh, we would love to have this house, Mom. We kind of talked about it when you and Jack left. It would be perfect for us."

"It's settled then, we all have new houses," Sam said happily. "I will miss this house. It has so many memories for me, it's where I learned to live again. After you and your brothers had grown up and went to college, I was lonely by myself. But here I felt at home, and this is where I found Jack. It is sentimental to me, so knowing that you will now have this house makes me incredibly happy, Sabrina. So, let's talk about your wedding plans, Sabrina. Tell us what you two are planning," Sam said sitting at the table, eyeing the magazine pictures that were strewn all over the table.

Sabrina talked breathlessly about the kind of wedding they wanted. They wanted to keep it small and simple with family and some friends. They asked Jack if they could use the restaurant like Nick and Sarah had, and Kevin, and Kali's planned for their upcoming wedding. Jack was truly honored to have them ask to have the wedding there.

"Since Jack is on board with us using his restaurant, like my brothers before me, this part may sound crazy, but hear us out, OK?" Sabrina said.

Jack and Sam looked at each other and nodded their heads.

"Freddie and I have given this crazy idea a lot of thought. I already called Kevin on this. He is on board too."

"Oh, dear Lord, Sabrina," Sam chuckled.

"Kevin and Kali are getting married Memorial Day weekend, right? So we thought we would have our wedding the day after theirs, since the restaurant will already be decorated for their wedding, it will be all set. We would all decorate it together and split the cost, what do you think?" Sabrina asked enthusiastically.

"Wow that is quite a plan. Are you sure that is what you really want?" Sam asked.

"Yes, we really do. I know I always wanted the big princess wedding but what I really want is just to marry the man I love. I don't need all the foo-foo and fluff." Sabrina said in air quotes.

"I think that is an excellent idea and if you want us to tweak anything after Kevin's wedding, I am sure we would be able to do that, Sabrina," Jack offered.

"Thanks, Jack, we want to keep it simple. Kevin and Kali are, too, so the four of us can figure it out together. It will be even more special." She beamed.

"Sounds like a lovely idea. Then we should start dress shopping soon, Sabrina," Sam giggled.

"Absolutely, Mom. And maybe you could find a dress too."

"You should look for a dress, Sam, that would be fun for you both," Jack said.

"Jack, we don't even have our date picked yet, besides I don't want to take away from Sabrina's shopping day."

"Oh, Mom, it would be so fun to shop together, but you can't buy the same dress as me," Sabrina giggled.

"OK maybe I will look too, but Jack when do you want to get married?" she asked him.

"Tomorrow," he laughed.

"That's sweet but I don't think we could, that's too soon." Sam smiled at him.

"Let's have dinner and you two can think it over," Freddie suggested.

"Sounds good. I am starving," Jack said.

They cleared the table of all the wedding paraphernalia. They enjoyed the delicious dinner that Freddie and Sabrina had made. They enjoyed lively conversation about wedding décor, dresses, and flowers. After the dishes were done and put away, Jack asked Sam if she wanted to go watch the sunset. He brought a blanket and some wine and grabbed her hand. It was a little chilly, so Sam grabbed their jackets.

"What a great meal. Freddie is really an amazing cook; no help from Sabrina I might add," Sam chuckled.

"I taught that boy everything he knows." Jack winked at her.

"I have no doubt he learned a lot from you, Jack. You have been like a father to him for so many years."

"He truly has been like a son to me. I am lucky to have him in my life like that, and that he is such a good, hard worker, too. I feel very confident letting him run that restaurant. He probably won't even need me," Jack chuckled.

"So, Sam, have you given any more thought to setting our wedding date now that Sabrina and Freddie are all set with their date and planning?"

"Well, I had a thought. What if we had our wedding at our new beach house?" Sam smiled at him.

"Oh, that's a fantastic idea, Sam. The back patio would be absolutely beautiful," he agreed.

"How long will it take to get into the new house?"

"Well, after the paperwork is done for the offer and being that they already accepted it, I would imagine only a couple of months," he said.

"OK that puts us into May, too close to Sabrina and Kevin's weekend, so what if we get married on the Fourth of July? We can have everyone stay here at the house and have a cookout and fireworks," she said enthusiastically.

"Oh, I love that idea, Sam. That would be a lot of fun. It's set then. On the Fourth of July at our new beach house, with family and friends, a cookout, and fireworks. It sounds perfect, Sam."

"It is perfect because we will finally be married. I love you, Jack."

"I love you, my sweet, sweet Sam."

Chapter 16

The next few months flew by with wedding dress shopping for both Sabrina and Samantha. Sabrina had chosen a beautiful strapless satin sheath dress. Samantha chose a simple knee-length, strapless lace dress. Since it wasn't going to be a formal event, Sam wanted a dress she could wear comfortably all day.

Sabrina worked with Kevin and Kali on the decorations for the restaurant for their combo wedding weekend.

Jack and Sam kept busy with their new beach house. They packed up the things Sam wanted to take to the new house. Sabrina and Freddie were so appreciative of the paintings and furniture Sam left for the young couple. Sam and Jack moved into their new home at the beginning of May. Freddie had moved into the beach house with Sabrina.

Before they knew it, it was Memorial Day weekend. Nick and Sarah arrived and were surprised by a baby shower that they had all planned for them. Both weddings went smoothly that weekend. It was a smooth transition from Kevin's wedding to Sabrina's wedding the following day. It truly was a magical moment for Sam seeing the last two of her children married. It brought her so much joy and happiness.

Before she knew it, it was the Fourth of July weekend. She was sitting on the back patio which overlooked the never-ending view of the beach. It was a view of beauty that just never ended. Jack joined her, grabbed her hand, and kissed the back of it.

"How is my sweet, sweet bride doing on this beautiful wedding morning?" he asked her.

"I am absolutely positively over the moon happy." She smiled at him.

"Me too. We have waited a long time for this day. I have dreamed of it myself all the time. I know we have been through so much life already, but I'm so thankful we found each other again to live out the rest of this life together and grow old together," Jack said with tears in his eyes.

"I feel the same way. You were my first love; my heart has always belonged to you, Jack."

They sat there holding hands for a long time until Sabrina came in, in her usual enthusiastic style.

"OK, Mom, time to get you ready for this beautiful wedding," she sang.

Sam stood and hugged Jack goodbye. "See you at the trellis, Jack," she giggled to him.

He kissed her cheek and said "I will be there waiting, waiting with open arms, eagerly for my sweet, sweet Sam."

Jack and Sam said their vows with family and friends surrounding them. Sam couldn't believe she was actually getting married to Jack. Her life was truly blessed. As they were announced, Mr. and Mrs. fireworks were exploding over the ocean. Beautiful sprays of colors and loud pops that thrilled them all.

Samantha and Jack were finally married thirty years after meeting each other that beautiful summer when they were young teenagers. They both had loved, and lost loves, but their love carried them through the riptides of life's ups and downs.

About the Author

Shelley Hibbard, a native of Upstate NY, is an author inspired by her love for the ocean and beach. Her passion for exploring the world is reflected in her activities, which include camping, traveling, and biking. When not adventuring, Shelley cherishes time with her family, which has a profound influence on her writing. This love for family and adventure has culminated in her creation of *The Ocean III*, a captivating blend of love story and mystery. Her work is a testament to her experiences and passions, appealing to readers who share her love for exploration and strong family bonds.

www.ingramcontent.com/pod-product-compliance
Lightning Source LLC
LaVergne TN
LVHW092058060526
838201LV00047B/1445